First published 2012 by Parragon Books, Ltd.

Copyright © 2018 Cottage Door Press, LLC
5005 Newport Drive
Rolling Meadows, Illinois 60008

ISBN: 978-1-68052-450-5

Parragon Books is an imprint of Cottage Door Press, LLC.
Parragon Books® and the Parragon® logo are
registered trademarks of Cottage Door Press, LLC.

The Three Little Pigs

Retold by Kath Jewitt

Illustrated by Mei Matsuoka

PaRRagon.

Once upon a time, there were three little pigs who lived in a cozy cottage on the hill.

They loved to eat all the delicious food their mother made them every day. They ate so much, that it wasn't long before the three little pigs had grown so big that there was no room for them in the cozy cottage any more.

"I'm sorry," said their mother one morning, "but it's time you made your own way in the world."

So the very next day, the three little pigs left home.

"Don't forget to watch out for the Big Bad Wolf," called their mother, as she waved goodbye. "He'll eat you for supper, so you'll need to build a big, fine, strong house as quickly as you can to keep him away."

"Don't worry, Ma!" they oinked. "We can look after ourselves!"

And the three little pigs trotted off down the hill, each taking a different path.

It wasn't long before the first little pig met a farmer pulling a cart filled with straw.

"Please may I buy some straw to build a house?" asked the little pig.

"Of course," replied the farmer, "but a straw house won't be very strong!"

But the little pig didn't listen. Soon he was busy stacking the bundles of straw for his new house.

In no time at all, the house of
straw was finished, and the little
pig went inside for a nap.

He had just shut his eyes, when
there was a knock at the door.

It was the Big Bad Wolf. And he was hungry!

"Little pig, little pig, let me in!" growled the wolf.

"No!" cried the little pig. "Not by the hair on my chinny-chin-chin!"

"Then I'll HUFF… and I'll PUFF… and I'll blow your house down!" laughed the wolf. And that's just what he did.

HUFF! PUFF! WHOOSH!

Meanwhile, the second little pig was
walking along the road when he saw
a woodcutter, piling up sticks.

"Please may I buy some sticks?" he asked
politely. "I want to build a house."

"Of course," answered the woodcutter, "but a
house made of sticks will soon fall down!"

But the second little pig wasn't listening. He was much too busy planning his new stick home.

Soon the house was finished. The little pig had just sat down to rest, when there was a knock at the door.

It was the Big Bad Wolf. He was even hungrier now!

"Little pig, little pig, let me in!" he growled.

"No way! Not by the hair on my chinny-chin-chin!" cried the second little pig.

"Then I'll HUFF… and I'll PUFF… and I'll blow your house down!" cried the wolf. And that's exactly what he did.

HUFF! PUFF! WHOOSH!

Meanwhile, the third little pig had met a builder.

"Please may I buy some of your bricks to build my house?" he asked.

"Of course," replied the builder. "A fine, strong house of bricks will last forever!"

The third little pig took the builder's advice. He would build the strongest house in the land!

Finally, after a hard day's work, the house was finished. It had four strong walls of brick, a tiled roof, a sturdy wooden door, and a large fireplace with a chimney.

The third little pig had just put a pot of turnips on the fire to boil, when he saw his brothers running down the road—closely followed by the Big Bad Wolf.

"Quick!" cried the third little pig. "Hide in here!"

The wolf, who was very hungry by now,
banged on the sturdy front door.

"Little pigs, little pigs, let me in!" he growled, his tummy rumbling very loudly with hunger.

"No way! Not by the hairs on our chinny-chin-chins!" cried the three little pigs.

"Then I'll HUFF… and I'll PUFF… and I'll blow your house down!" laughed the wolf.

So he HUFFED...
and he PUFFED...

and he PUFFED...
and he HUFFED...

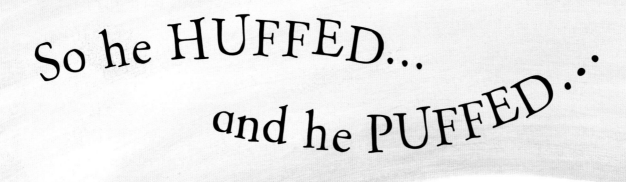

But the brick house stood firm.

The wolf was furious! He climbed up onto the roof and shouted down the chimney.

"If I can't blow your house down, I'll come down the chimney and gobble you all up!"

The Big Bad Wolf jumped and landed with a huge
SPLASH! in the pot of turnips boiling on the fire below.

EEEEEEEYOWWWW!

He leaped up with
a scream and ran out
of the house, never to
be seen again.

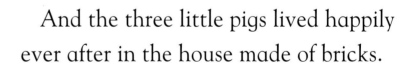

And the three little pigs lived happily
ever after in the house made of bricks.

The End